D1463086

AND FOR EXAMPLE

ALSO BY
ANN LAUTERBACH

Clamor

Before Recollection

Greeks
(with Bruce Boice and Jan Groover)

Many Times, But Then

ANN LAUTERBACH

AND FOR EXAMPLE

PENGUIN POETS

PENGUIN BOOKS
Published by the Penguin Group
Penguin Books USA Inc., 375 Hudson Street, New York, New York 10014, U.S.A.
Penguin Books Ltd, 27 Wrights Lane, London W8 5TZ, England
Penguin Books Australia Ltd, Ringwood, Victoria, Australia
Penguin Books Canada Ltd, 10 Alcorn Avenue,
Toronto, Ontario, Canada M4V 3B2
Penguin Books (N.Z.) Ltd, 182–190 Wairau Road,
Auckland 10, New Zealand

Penguin Books Ltd, Registered Offices: Harmondsworth, Middlesex, England

First published in simultaneous hardcover and
paperback editions by Penguin Books 1994

1 3 5 7 9 10 8 6 4 2

Copyright © Ann Lauterbach, 1994
All rights reserved

Page ix constitutes an extension of this copyright page.

LIBRARY OF CONGRESS CATALOGING IN PUBLICATION DATA
Lauterbach, Ann, 1942–
And for example : poems / Ann Lauterbach.
p. cm.—(Penguin poets)
ISBN 0-670-85883-8 (hc.)
ISBN 0 14 058.715 2 (pbk.)
I. Title.
PS3562.A844A83 1994
811'.54—dc20   94-5814

Printed in the United States of America
Set in Bembo
Designed by Katy Riegel

Without limiting the rights under copyright reserved above, no part of this publication may be reproduced, stored in or introduced into a retrieval system, or transmitted, in any form or by any means (electronic, mechanical, photo-copying, recording or otherwise), without the prior written permission of both the copyright owner and the above publisher of this book.

Except in the United States of America, this book is sold subject to the condition that it shall not, by way of trade or otherwise, be lent, re-sold, hired out, or otherwise circulated without the publisher's prior consent in any form of binding or cover other than that in which it is published and without a similar condition including this condition being imposed on the subsequent purchaser.

To Joe Brainard
—*I remember*

and for my brother, David

Acknowledgment is made to the following publications, in which some of the poems in this book (sometimes in earlier drafts) originally appeared:

Annandale: "Fabric (Remnant Light)"; *The American Poetry Review:* "The Prior"; *Big Allis:* "Seven Songs for Joe"; *Conjunctions:* "Rancor of the Empirical," "The Scene Shifts," "The Untelling," "Tangled Reliquary," "Ashes, Ashes," "In the Museum of the Word"; *Denver Review:* "Eclipse with Object," "Rapture of the Spoken"; *The Global City Review:* "Harm's Way, Arm's Reach," "The Tacit"; *New American Writing:* "And the Fire Spread"; *Notus:* "Of the Fire"; *oblēk:* "Stepping Out"; *Ploughshares:* "Song of the Already Sung"; *Promethean:* "Song of the Anchor (Penelope)"; *Voice Literary Supplement:* "Missing Ages."

"Poem (with Postcard from Vermont)" first appeared in *That Various Field for James Schuyler,* edited by William Corbett and Geoffrey Young (Great Barrington, Mass.: The Figures, 1991).

We ought to say a feeling of *and*, a feeling of *if*, a feeling of *but*, and a feeling of *by*, quite as readily as we say a feeling of *blue* or a feeling of *cold*.

—*William James*

Unto the Whole—how add?

—*Emily Dickinson*

The author wishes to express her gratitude to Nan Graham and Bradford Morrow for their encouragement and exceptional care, to The Corporation of Yaddo for timely time, to the John D. and Catherine T. MacArthur Foundation for endowing the possible, to Joshua Wilner, Paul Sherwin, Joan Richardson, and Joseph Wittreich for collegial friendship of the first order, and to her students for keeping the fire stoked.

Some of the language on pages 58–59 was drawn from a talk by Vito Acconci; the quotations on pages 66 and 67 are drawn from Ludwig Wittgenstein.

CONTENTS

AND FOR EXAMPLE

THE UNTELLING

ECLIPSE WITH OBJECT

There is a spectacle and something is added to history.
It has as its object an indiscretion: old age, a
gun, the prevention of sleep.

I am placed in its stead
and the requisite shadow is yours.
It casts across me, a violent coat.

It seems I fit into its sleeve.
So the body wanders.
Sometime it goes where light does not reach.

You recall how they moved in the moon dust? *Hop, hop.*
What they said to us from that distance was stupid.
They did not say *I love you* for example.

The spectacle has been placed in my room.
Can you hear its episode trailing,
pretending to be a thing with variegated wings?

Do you know the name of this thing?
It is a rubbing from an image.
The subject of the image is that which trespasses.

You are invited to watch. The body asleep
in complete dark casting nothing back.
The thing turns and flicks and opens.

RANCOR OF THE EMPIRICAL

A lavish pilgrim, her robes unbound,
checks into a nearby hotel.
Let us spread the wealth.
Let us speak in such a way
we are understood, as a shadow
is understood to assuage these prisms
and these mercurial clasps. She was told
yes and she was told *no*
which is how she became excessive, spilling
over the sequestered path, her wild garments
lacerating stones.
She took pills against rain.
She slept under tinfoil.
In that country, there were no heroes
to invent a way to fill the hours
with parables of longing, so her dreams
were blank. Sometimes she imagined
voices which led to her uneven gait
and to her partial song. Once she was seen
running. A child said he saw her fly
low over the back meadow and into the pines, her
feet *raving in wind*. The child
was punished for lying, made to eat ashes
in front of the congregation. The priest said,
You have made a petty story. Now enter duration.

THE PRIOR

1.

Edge of a lot vacant, wishing for that.
Covetous of what the afternoon would bring.

An errand the mind might run.

Something to do after the holiday; a spree.

After the holiday and all, still hungry.
Something worthy of news: that not tame.

In the film it was evident
there was nothing to tell. You could tell
that. Only spillage, only excess
as a form of boredom. Her breasts
and tall legs all decked out; lips
formatted *kiss*. His
mouth aroused by vacancy.
Streets tricked out in garbage but
no particular scent in blue air.

Something to do after the ride back on Friday.

You could tell you were moving away
from what you owned. No one knew
what to call the next one, only
that it would come and it would be the same.
Same and silent, an anonymous likeness.
Wanting to say this is not the same
this is not the same as *this*.

Walking across the bridge,
a fictive suspense.

Things are delivered, too many
to keep safely, to follow as the hymnal
word for word. Tune sullied by disuse;
chimes bricked up. The assumed
enclosure in need of repair.

2.

Striking out into the calamity
quest without caption

here take this highly influential ingot
this jacket, book, odd velvet

props left out over there
kept offscreen at any distance

hung from a single chain
sad stamina of the scene

a common thing
not a list, not an emblem, not required

financed by a steady gaze
the boy's bright gaze in the bright air

his mate might come with her cats
(unreliable cats on the church roof)

a slack wind and a catastrophic sail
Ditto said the boy, the Dante, learning.

3.

If this were speech, a speech
could it elicit the X mentioned above
of which this might be the result?
They were only playing.
Mask without face, no real tears
under the obligatory smile. Real anything.
Examples could be footsteps following the real.
He drew a thread on a wall, not architecture,
so when we looked back only bending, shifting.
Bending, shifting, usual noise, kids
yelling in twilight, tired from the sun.
They are waiting to be told to come in. *I said now.*
I said now they are waiting to be told to come in.

What is it based on what pleasure
what lost in what of your own making—

enclosure needs repair.
Boat without sail. Many tourists.

THE SCENE SHIFTS

Things inhabited recalled as stark.
There is; there *it* is. And now
swerve, asking to be
located or found out, arms lifted—

had he known he would have said so. I
am nearing it for you, on your behalf.
Please follow. What was said was
in answer to what was forgotten, the blond
who visited yesterday is dead, was
then. She was an incursion
on what he knew, seeing her.
Seeing her, he wanted her name.
Tina? Daisy? The mad woman
repeated in the hall—*Hear that? A*
mad woman!—where the stench awaited
consummation. It was available like a list.
Across from the cathedral
the list was in a hall,
in some stripped mirage of *next, next.*
Another sits in a kindred reverie
as a child picks up a shell
and wishes to be absorbed into its socket.
Daisy is happy to have
married to have coupled with November
in the low island light speckled with chronology.
Tina is dead. What it was he came to call her
spilled as if it were salt. It was not salt.

The revered, the pagan annulment, the lark
with consequences: *boom, boom.*

Try talking of it in your sleep
when there's no one around to hear.
Once she thought she was a banner
above a statue
in one of those parks you read about.
I used to live across from that park.
Then all things became absorbed
into one, like a continent,
rooted in adages, portrayed on stamps.
She is walking around with a sure sense
that this is the later they were
trying to imagine when they said
it would be like this. Some
are sitting elsewhere
in a kingdom with stiff fines for leaving.
The kingdom is small and has no king.

SONG OF THE ANCHOR (PENELOPE)

From among many
availed, coastal

        this gown

I gave him
sea's ragged lace

        white spume

eager to be swallowed
to cruise at his shoulder/his eye
casting for land

        mast set

          sail all out

fueled by
speed of nothing
the most ancient nothing.

        While in the harbor
folded, scented with yarn
someone weaves on wood

        apricot boughs

fish swayed in nets
things drying

        dry weeds gathered in bunches

      lavender, sage

        resting on my back

on blue facing blue
and a long rope of something entangled below
descending like metal

        like blood from a cut—

scald said to the image *scald scald.*

GREEN TALISMAN

to Dominique Fourcade

Beauties may await us
the sunset is brittle

hesitant, replicating
all things nude in recovery

surrounded by brothers and
further sad-eyed estrangements

each transmitted
carefully

miraculous or glad
respite then, then

sung between letters
tallow nub

new growth fluid *avec*
vocal with speed

as by prayer
tidily excelled

companionable touch
after fever

plume or ribbon
dormez-vous?

placed in kind above all hours
below each incursion in variegated slant.

RAPTURE OF THE SPOKEN

Faced with so many/nothing framed
creamy dialectic of the ungood

This one's for sale/this not
save your pennies for later

Shelter's precision disengaged
chronic singularity, chronic behavior

How not to spend the day
how not to dream

When to wait your turn on the swing.
                              Prelude
to a longer sequence
which already occurred in the home: you
wanted to learn
the consesquences of this much consequence
when the pictures came back framed.
                    The first touch
scared you when it first appeared
as image: a man in a park says
your eyes are beautiful and this
became a question the body could not answer.
If you stay on the threshold
you might become a saint, you could pass the cup.
Years later, the brush leaves its mark
overtly, like a kiss.
But the picture does not respond.
The picture goes on staring at the morning.

THE UNTELLING

The task subsides, gloating in perpetuity. This
without watching, a form of purpose
exhaled, possibly spoken.

Because of the length of knowing
valued in the first place, its name
unattached from the rigors of display,
withheld as *later*, as *before* or *after*.

Then you say
tell me and tell again
and I say

The leaves are a wall.

And she came down the stairs
intentionally.

And then the man the end.

So that later it seemed a season had landed.
And you ask *which which*
and what is it about?

Down the stairs where the irretrievables
were kept. Or: her purple shoes
are in the dollhouse. Or:

it came as if pulled slowly
as a mouth filled with awe

moves its silence slowly in a ring.
Only a picture could picture it.

And you ask
was it a kiss that did not happen on any street
to her so it did not predict, make amends,
was not an extra key, a visit?

I repeat *the leaves are a wall.*

Explain you say.

I say jewels sprawl before the Rat Man.
I say Cassandra at her dusty ball
her old mouth saying *what what*
put your house in order
the people are turning away
I see fire in heaps
I see air perpetually stale
I see a stiff patch shifting.

Explain you say.

I say someone I do not know told me
my Godfather Tom
was found
on 57th Street
in a dumpster. Tom
she said looked like Walt Whitman
with a beard and long filthy nails.
He was the theatre editor of LIFE
magazine during its heyday. He
took me to see *Waiting for Godot.* He
gave me a book on Etruscan art
a dragon from Nepal

a round-trip ticket to Paris. He said
you are an eagle behaving like a beetle.

You say
the wall is on the ground
thank you good-bye.

UNDER COVER OF DARKNESS

In the park it was lovely that day, you recall?
I had the night off, and the hour began with you
saying *hi* like a hero in a film we had not seen.
I thought
how will I continue to chat
when this is here, in the flesh,
this *music*.

                    (music fills space)

After that season, we met again in the woods
of the corner Korean store, where the flowers are.
The night was not young, but
then, no time is.
Love all you want, history still
prevails with its ugly show.
This year, we must arrange for a kiss.
Forebears, influences are published at a leisurely pace
although soon everything will be made in China,
where industry *is* romance.
Remote fashions are born that cleave
and resemble, but who says what is forgotten?
The cloudy clocks, purloined from a script,
hunch into guns, shoot their rays, thousands die.
We trade this chromosome for that, knowing
it recovers so easily from what ails—

condensed into Western standards:
one woman and one man at
different speeds.

And the steps of November are heard
late into the evening which the garland left
as a requiem one Sunday during a different performance
in New York. Did you want to exchange it for another?
Beloved, the drums are within hearing
although the wind is not.
Before I die I intend to tell you these things.
Bitter hair in the drain, remains

of a nest, but other couplings
have come undone, have
turned to salt in exile.
The long paths require our stillness
and separate, one going off to the next season
the other halted at the moon.

We drove as if
chasing the zodiac, making a road of night air, its
zero equation, its vertiginous shelf.
Cables of denial bind us to such strangeness
we grope, prisoners
of persistence, for hope's lethal circuit.
Not even food gets in. Everything else is in transit.

THE TACIT

Look how torpid, how in uncanny knack we
desire aversion.
The train will not switch tracks.
Nor any able spy, any sequence thus plumbed.
Look how I eye your profile
and announce a wish to apply my wish
that is, to conclude.

We could be former, estranged, then not know
even our fingers, forget
how ample the tongue is in its own language.
A ceremony would then pronounce us.
There would be a sense a watch had fallen
into a river. There would be those
birds, the ones with red flashing,
chasing in low bushes by water. There would be
enthusiasm, as of many days
folded into one promenade, one terrace or font.

You could say I live now
in this avuncular tree, and that house must
vanish because I loved once too often, or twice
or for life.

Woman spoon, timeless clock, man
capsizing in perpetuity.
An uneasiness. Webern's Opus five.

POEM
(WITH POSTCARD FROM VERMONT)

to James Schuyler

To resist
cluster, to become
scaffold's deceptive inch
wanting its incident

signatures of intimate light imported
wherein we are held

       And the arcade's last seeming
down by the edge of a visitor's eye, voice
purloined from its knowledge, discursive,
fleet: that side of the street, its relation
to this.

Daylilies furled
         withered flags (farewell! farewell!)
         erect pointers (hello!)

         say the redolent near

I think of the weight of your thighs
and want the day to speak in their trace
to build a new tower for the children to watch

         riding the sky
         first one hawk, then another
         high, sad whistle
         as for a lost dog

Now coming around the corner

           sole brown duck
           car with broken exhaust pipe

"only realism can't be proven by means of it"
yet it is raining
slowly enough
to count.

A certain but animate diction
some belong to, are claimed by
tossed into seeds others may follow

blur of periwinkles, casket
of Queen Anne's lace

last seen on a curb, like
Baudelaire's *flâneur,*
impossible to translate

and now robed in remorse but not cloudy
down the aisle, the aisle, the—

Dear Jimmy:

last night Kenward, Joe and I
drove to Greensboro
to see Beverly and Bill
on the hill above the lake
(the view as giant postcard of itself)
some green fields in the shape of an angel dancing—

Now it is raining faster.

SEVEN SONGS FOR JOE

1.

Already the air

has no sleeve.
The top and bottom

are charmless.
And the turn, already,
into

an array

concealed
or skipped over

where June was.

Already the stair

is awash
with cherries is

a sled
on rocks.

2.

In the bin below Athens
a trove
broken into shards

              the signed figured
              vase has
              value

stored in tins
cisterns

              Dionysus is drinking/the Macedonians
              wore this hat

              a mixture of wine
              and water

vats
large vessels
amphorae

              a common object
              it has less value
              when it loses its context

the deposits are closed
the nucleus is abandoned

the messy debris
under Athens.

3.

In a list of fires:
world fire, world fire II,
fire in America

vestal fire
Gondwana fire
Burning Bush.

4.

There is
a
button on
the rug there
is
a button
on the rug
there
is a
button
on the rug
there is a
button on the
rug. Rug.

5.

Halloween eve/walked
under the moon

          jumping
      how now
shed
   Armani mask
          dredged
into black
hound's tooth
rain

Vintage epicurean knot knows no
spindle, no thread

homespun
comes down, dips

            in the pond's palm   broken
                    handle of vase
                    splash of stars

                                        pours out

and
over there the herald is
still golden, recently
returned from his contract
and the natty author
and the tan.
Beautiful young men
are brought forward
extending their flesh
and
and
are told
to listen to the humdrum
catastrophic
street.
Day into night
colder by inches
and
those who are told
start to sing.

6.

A ring is in the wilderness.
It is divorced.

                    In the pavement
stonily clad, excluded
from a hand.
Trammel of a carriage, of
wheels without nerve tracking the path

whose entire
makes itself memory

                                        come back! come back thief!
vagrant ring
bent into
leftover silvers, wild pearls, foraging needles, print, petals

                    ungathered
                                        an immense yellow hauls
its timetable
across a day's
naked throat

combs
fall from the sea

bees
nest in mud.

In the first place
there was no Radio City,
no recalled stuff
no Cadillac,
no wife Marie.
This passionate loam ebbtide sensation
wasn't it swift?

Boy leaning on brick
the goddess exploding
the ample ruin in the yard.

Now instead a doctrine
of old twilights cast
into our river
scrolls with fevered lists

subtracted

and a glider alights
in far-off sands, its
wings'

incandescent rattle
as the narrative staff
presses its period
(in binding fortune) away.

7.

You with a garden at your feet—lilies
and small red roses, iris—all
out of season in glass vases
on steps

     as if
you had said
it is enough

not to have desire
but for how the day folds open

small napkin
on a wide table

                                       we will unwed our sisters
graduate
into little anarchies of dawn

so sham
there will be

only replicas.
What shall we do with the day?

FABRIC (REMNANT LIGHT)

The day's   and of this beware: heat
        and is incontinent. Much that is
is   intact,
coming dreamily to roost on the   plane
tomorrow blithe and mostly

Dark palisades of this after this.

                bells compete, weave
indeterminate claims (their
) while wide-eyed cherubs
        into the forest to find a

But is this   mine, a portion or
And have you   tell you   I know
or to   I come
or that I do not   Virtue
        a shadow up over a stranded   all
    suffused   as a favorite glass
            with chance.   A series of referrals
and then   certainty weighted against thirst.
The   is ancient and belongs   ancient

But whose   bears toward us
this   heavier
than we might have   Chance
a category?
I see gathered   chambers of indifference
a small crowd   in merest
of
                insatiable
at its orgy.

      So girl
delicate wrist inscribed
silver thread   throat. Kin
prays for kin. The man who   fish
at the local   handsome   landlord's
      is pregnant, she feels   The specific
      your hand might pass
to unfluctuate the night.
As if all
in a flicker of
then grief, then
then the implausible   thief
A vocabulary   through   stains   stain.

FOR EXAMPLE

These are examples of leaving out.
—*John Ashbery*

FOR EXAMPLE (1):
STEPPING OUT

It has been easy to say in recent times that everything tends to become real, or rather, that everything moves in the direction of reality, that is to say, in the direction of fact.

—*Wallace Stevens*

If everything tends to become real
then whose trial has ended
on a scale of one to ten
in which three is a dream
on a floor
no one can see.
                    Also, perhaps, maybe
elicit the shard from its fervor
to display amnesia: one person in jail
another walking across a roof
where what is written on the sky
brings formality to the event, as when
we first ask, *What is it?* The world,
loosed like a hem, is
what we step out on
and are pulled along away from our doors
not so much appeased as grafted
onto the long dark pause.
Pointing, not seeing anything, not knowing
the name for what isn't there.

But the prestige of a moment is not its name.
After all, we sleep among secrets

and wake to their burden.
If we could pay attention at all points then
theory would be what really is there. But then
another intimacy begins
while a chorus of male voices
carries the bar away/raft
of flowers brought into a girl/her body
emerging from the story as a new link
on an old sheet/ignorant single ambition of one hero
listening to another but not listening to this spring's snow.
Only the women speak of war, for example.
"To be prolonged in the first place
so we dream of escape," she said
in the midst of history.

                        The dictionary
is part of the clutter
lure, decoy, bait, snare, trap
and so to cross the heart
might make us *only here* or *here only*
depending on the translation.
Was one aflame? Is this a lake?
And why is part of the flower
mentioned at night
when she finds these love knots
in another dream she cannot recall. And
around the sinuous thread the doctor
with his pen
draws a line across her abdomen like the general
in the green room with his green map and stick, his
war game of war under the strong light of the canonical:
Kafka, Freud, and whatever girls might make an example.
Festering green bar, nothing on the menu available.
Et peut-être yes! now she understands why
she would rather not mention names
but what was it said of the singular? The wall

could be a *lining* or an *inner partition*
if everything tends to become real.

It's true, I was sad all day
for no good reason like a forgotten task
attached to too many site-specific verbs—
to want, desire, wish, require, please, try, attempt—
you get the idea. Only the finality of rhythm
on which to insist: rhythm as the example.
Now the resourceful writer becomes a drunk
as she stands against a church wall
under clear light.
Nothing is early enough, for example.
We are not located in the world but in its
particulars: what's done is done, the show is down.
Tyranny comes naturally to the dead. Was that
the perilous night
mentioned by the composer and copied
onto a page? The fat belly revealed, the wound
similar but not the same. Indifference
spoils what is real, for example.

So we find ourselves in the excess
of what is already here
and want to speed up to the good parts.
Some noises are glamorous, like dance, the
discipline of celebrated silence,
but love moans and collapses
under a saturated roof
and we admit to being ruined, at least once.
The glassy eye is anointed by its tear.
If you save everything that has hurt you, you
might come close to saying its prayer
passing the basket from hand to hand
not having to memorize the empty gaze

where you just were. Then
survival could be negative space
where what might be reconstructed
has fallen away beyond erasure
to the small case before travel.
Get back in your room.
Is anything in childhood mutual? The lifted
parameters of touch mingled with the stung
as when reaching up above clover
to the magics of another season
which might be serene. They danced
under an awful light, and her shoes, her gowns,
twisted in shadow; only the shadow has lasted.
The clasp of his hands on her back, for example.
The limbs of the corridor could not speak
but were folded under
where wet hair was out of sequence
on the black floor. The train
pulled its litany across a populous tread, torn
into geography and a wish to stay up later
than time, when whatever *wisteria* was would
bloom and hand down its scented ladder.
On that side of the street the boys were
always ready, but the stairs were dangerous and locked.
To protect what is new, to laugh without ambush or cartoon;
to sleep safely. It is a matter of listening, and so
learn how to depart. What is dragged behind is a
sound that is not understood, as the city
gathers and gathers, near
as what will not come back.

From up here in the bleachers
things seem real, but provisional, like a day
in which only paper airplanes sail by
to eventually cover the field.

Unfolded and flattened, they reveal
notes and pictures in colored pencil: hearts,
trees, flowers, rhyming couplets, and other
impediments of the age. And perhaps the game is
halted on account of this weather, which is only
the missing voice and truant litter of desire.
The athletes' faces hiss with sweat and rage
and Mom is picking up socks
and spare change, paying bills, lifting
the nearly empty carton of milk
off the shelf in the fridge. Her task
is to remember whatever comes next.
To her, time is an all too gregarious
protagonist, not so much eager to please as
insistent and daft, adept at charming the room
full of anxious initiates into voting his way
without knowing the facts, for example.
She thinks how rain on the roof
does sound like applause as she closes the windows.
By now the airplanes are mush
and the fans have departed in their vivid multicolored slickers
and hats. It seems strange to think
each knows where to go, although some may not get there.
Whereas all stories seemed false now
all seemed true; the confusion
was arbitrary. This spot, this
dime. She turns on the shadow of a breath
like a bird on a branch. *Touch me not*
was how it sounded from across the field, a page
torn from a journal in which she confessed
she could not wait, writing into the wait.

Maybe all absences should be excused.
The banquet, in any case, was dull;
the soufflé never rose. But things

fall on a regular basis, especially in spring,
and sometimes we hear them, petal by petal,
as when we put our ear to the chest
where the letters are kept.
Be sure to put the broken glass
in a brown paper bag so it won't cut
someone's hand; there's enough blood
in the carpet and in the sand. Even
the mattress is stained and, like sand,
indented with the shadow of weight.
This represents a decade of dreams
which also should be put in a sack or box
and shipped to a new address: strange,
how the body takes its dreams with it
like a city buried under the rubble of ages
never to be found. Strange, too,
how what is and what is not
make a quixotic braid
which, like weather, has no end
other than those we invent
to measure change. Rain again today.
You can hear it too, sloshing through the gutter
like a rope of sound. Instead of falling
you could walk downstairs
onto the familiar street, but be careful
and take your umbrella: remember, the street
won't miss you. It goes one way.

FOR EXAMPLE (2):
TANGLED RELIQUARY

to PG

Tangled reliquary under all surfaces.
Nothing moon-like occurs there
only partial coves
and entrances.
How cool it must have been
in the vat of the previous
before these habits ordained the real.
Some of us must have seen each other
naked in opulent dawn, our nerves
drawn up as from an ancient well
mossy, slick, unstuck at every seam
so we enter the sleeve of history
out of which the magician pulls
his lawn ornaments: Dancer, Prancer,

Our Lady of Provocation, flags, targets,
the bluebird's house.
                              On the adjacent field
a swarm of butterflies alights
in a bald tree. This is the Tree of Change
mentioned in the lost book of A.
Her auspice was a riddle, sphinx or no
sphinx, whose meanings we can piece together
from her journals that were torn into bandages
to wrap the wounds of the dying.
Such wanton songs paginate
empirical trust and the ruse of the first place.

Not that story, the one we cannot tell
to the sun as it dispenses its sheen

out over the harbor, but only
how can you perform your agile sway
without shelter and without us?
So the riddle of the disembodied name
sets in motion a primal mischief
sanctioned and forbidden in the vastly gone.

This would be a good day to go sailing
or to wash the car, but I have
neither boat nor car. There's a plotless
web in the air like a banner pulling us along
into something to look back on. What
if I wandered so far
only to come here

to the relentless
you have kept in store for me
before the song, above the river,
all the names etched in stone
only slowly annealed to the
spawning wind, in whose face
we will soon be included, having been shown
the near field's shambles
and grace. *Come here*
like a shoulder or a girl's skipping step
toward evening on a Friday—lapis amulet,
Samurai sword, Chinese silk stained with azalea,
a single earring the color of a toy globe—all
stolen from a thing called April

still wet with fresh rending. *Come
here* in a language

once learned, only a few phrases still known:
bonjour, je t'aime, il fait beau.

Perhaps one of those popular, musical Sundays
would save us, galloping at high speed in, out,
with a glimpse from up high
at the revised setting crowded with tyranny.
So I wanted *once again* as a plaything, some jewel, box, horse
on which to come fleet of vision, glad to pretend.
The cartoons sailed against the brocade and the stairs
were where the prayers were kept
like instruments of torture, basking

in shade, scent of new snow, locks of hair
under glass.
          The day, however,
has spun upwards so it seems to be a sort of chapel
of divided light, and the season, punctured,
leaks down on us as from a faint dead planet.
And I had promised never again to try to put
anything back together, to obey
the errant barge of upheavals, not to seek
cause and effect in the prevailing wind. But now
shards of promise glint through a network of uneven shifts
like the wandering voice of an ancestor
on the far side of the dunes. Bricks or dunes.
But what will we tell the children? As in a photo of

two persons dancing, there are some things
we never hear. *Shout coo shout coo*
each of us not there. So one who is the one
sheathes me in his ear. Him sings his tunes
in aberrant remonstrance and I
agree to this fear he tells whose words
are what he cares to do. Both hands are up

not so much surrendered as bequeathed
to our common night. *Dear dream,*
will you assist us, give pause
to any and all of these lessons, take us, each,
into such fond technologies that the thigh's
spasmodic hum frees action as well as solace?
But the eye
is dialectical and unreasoned, its gown
disembodied because unsaid. The blue floor
calls itself June and wants to lay me down
on its shine of now
and peel off the shadows one by one
until I am it. Then sail into the air
sheet after sheet, this, that, here, there,
now, then, only as real as what follows.
That the balloon man lost his head
that the screen fell to the floor
in a heap of landscape

                such mornings

that the clay pot
lay in shards that the dry flowers were cast

across the rug—ancient seeds, crumbs—

                such mornings

and the light reached all the way into the dark
as if handing it forward from some child's grave/from the
coiled boundaries/from whatever captivity
we wish to sew into artifact
but which, like the light just named, eludes us, frail and pinioned
in the glossy tablets of alchemical reserve/that the elegy is
betrayed as the child follows her hand into its sanctuary and
touches the core and unriddles the riddle in the beckoning need
that the cluster of disavowal gives way
and could not be shy—

                such mornings—

FOR EXAMPLE (3): LOST SECTION

This *three* has been lost, twice. In the *mundane shell*, or some
wheel riding the *harrow*.

In the books there is not an adequate collection,
and her letters all ask for money, from some
corner of the Atlantic.

       She was told to make it up as she went along
as if it were part of nature.
That was before
the *infernal scroll*
closed over the tender moon (the moon
of the first and second version, both
now lost in terrains of clover and bleach
in the *mills, ovens, cauldrons*
of error).

The quotidian is not surrounded by heavenly invention;
an aged woman raves *along the streets.*
The key, kept at the far end of the porch, is hung
on a metal cask beyond the white plastic patio furniture
now covered with snow. It's a bright spring day
at the end of another year in which too much
was exposed, like fat flesh under a diva's robes.
Plot, according to Aristotle, is the soul of tragedy
but he fails to tell
what to do
after the end of the story.

None of this was in the first version.
I have forgotten the second.

What spills over into the blank? What form?
The text is rich where it shares this darkness.
This does not relate to an invisible wind.

Kept in the trunks of distant trees
it is not released by any key
poked into emptiness,
just as a song will not come forth from any mouth.

Understand: *I am in pursuit of the missing part.*
What I remember: foil, a loom,
a cot, cruelty,
wrappings, unwrappings,
gold embers, a robe—

        so the robe

opens on an orb
and the case is how we find our way
out of the privileged cast of night

      —I think
that's how it went. Then,

Put your ear to her mouth and ask her to sing.

      Tiny slip of moon
seen through the cage hurts
my eyes. How to teach what is arrested? Those
hill towns beckon from their height and the wall,
the high wall, calls from across an alley.
Hark! little door, little exit,
let me gather these boughs before they lose their scent.

Hunters move toward their prey all the way over to the other side
where the flame gives out.

It cold here.

Floating downstream/olive eyes
mounted above the amazed mouth of a monk/prophetic scar
angled toward earth
at the site of instruction

we are, after all
the one that speaks

as from behind the wall
quotation marks, agile as lashes, blind as bats
come to tell of the wreath. Truth? No, the wreath

—season now scrap now
glossed as such

its site
a doorknob and the hand that finds it
as when leaving is knowing when to leave
(train curving across the bridge back into the city)
and the sublime, with no example,
catapults into the silken net, O
river of scripts
presuming the endeavor is real.

Birds chipping away at dawn.
In the quarantine morning, a gentle pitter-patter of lapses.
If only we could become wise, if only we could
sleep with Athena.

                    And the magical boy, cool-fingered as a witch
stands on a glass palette, a nebula
of related shapes, not random, belonging to
something, to the same special case,
special *and* same
but hid from us as a new model forms from the old putrid stuff—

disease, commentary, foliage,
gargoyle, cup,
argument, reversal,
stipend, recognition, fate.

Yet there was a time when there were only
ripples coming in from a distant event so that,
standing at the window, something
baffles him. Is destination a tunnel, far
from ordinary experience? Something worries him,
some relic

            standing at the window
watching space bend in the wind's fabric
breaching the wave's hump

                            the figure turning now
back into the doorway's prescience—
And yet, there was a time when time was ripples
coming in from a distant event so that
standing in front of a window, something
worries him, some relic

standing at the window
watching space bend in the wind's fabric—

They were hoping to find bumps in this; it was a hope. If you blow up the
second resonance, it decays into more particles. When people do collisions and
find particles, what does it look like? Final decay.

—breaching the wave's hump.

                              The figure
turning back into the doorway as through
the lashing force, through, across, into
placing us in his esteem
ruptured, alert,
in the darkness of the dark's dark.
What comes next, *four, five, six,*
is what has not yet been counted, turning,
answering the door, letting it in.

                                        It cold here.

The curtains move.

Some wind.

FOR EXAMPLE (4):
ADRIFT ON A SUMMER'S DAY

What other? Fortune's rib? dress?
Every which way! and just in time for lunch.

                                   So much these days
is correctable, so much else
can be traded up
into the vertical, musical tide.
See the posies glittering in window boxes?
Hear the *thrum thrum* of a distant rave?
And he climbs up over the wall
into the city that wants him.
Blanket too thick for this season anyway.
Body too big for this room.
Here is a number for Dolores.
She must be pretty, if too thin.
If too thin she can be made fatter.
If too fat she too can climb the twilight
until she floats away.

                         Key to the wind-blown. Hello shift.
Are these *painted daisies* to your taste? Now
that the river has been separated from its bank
can you tell me where the cardboard is?
Hair all frizzy from rain.
Stain on my lapel where the train passed.
The gap is called *when morning fits*, folds
out into the mass.
                  Onto the dangerous hoopla
where something is

instead of the pivot: ready, set
or possibly not ready, no belt to hold
what widens into evening, what will be, has been,
forfeited. Was it the street's ode
or the young girl's diary, in which too much was tested
too soon? She felt inappropriate, dewy,
wishing Johnny would call. Later, she let down
her hair, *Rapunzel, Rapunzel,* into the gutter
lethal with boundaries: so.
And so noted the brew of birds, the blistery rasp
of frog-life. Sounds inimical to saying.

Once, there was a man who listened.
He was explicit, foreign. She
noticed him in the threshold, the shelter,
and was covetous, wanting so to lean.
Once, too, the glove fit its stupid sister
then one was lost, became a blur,
and trundled into musty books
where her eyes saw the image
but nothing in the background noticed it.
Therefore fiction fears us. She turns
to program notes, hopes something rhymes
or can be proven. Some are anointed, floral.
Others are objects merely, unscented.
She wonders which to kill, which favor:
salt, butcher's wax, peat moss, acid for the drain.
A great horse stood at the gate, marble from a distance,
something like perfection as when
the escalator brought her to his mouth.
If you believe in *seasons.* If you believe in *art.*
If not, elections are coming up
and we could always move to California.
Front yard, back yard. Barbecue pit.

See, the entourage insists, staring up at the window
where the star lived. The house is for sale,
the placard stiff in smoky air.

Meanwhile, a gloved hand
enters the pictorial frame and opens the city,
all illusion, decal, dance;
cellophane, cartoon, flimsy tunnels;
a camera's gray fluidity, ceaseless unfolding iconicity
sequential nearness and virtual—

There is no scent on these hands.
These heads have no hands.
There are no words on these pages

                    (white butterfly passes, torn from . . .)
                                    and could,
in future, call everything up,
turn it out, flat, onto the screen: you
with all your nodes, visions, climaxes,
your voice a sort of lilac with violet edges,
your hands, hair, nails, veins, gestures, reach,
watch them (in the small room, late spring,
Belmondo and the girl with short hair, air
tangled with French) aroused
by the story of the story's story,
rewind, watch, rewind, watch
so that nothing (everything) ends.

Plato's sun has shown us the fact of our chains.
A mauve cloud with pale pink edges
painted on water, on or in,
nothing resembles it
as it disrobes, exposes its skin, its

lessness. Saying, as the dark arrives,
stripping, naked and palpable, shifting now into now into—
let us begin.

                In time, she may also be the one with broken glasses
curled on a cot, soiled as in a history:
distraction without care, no one to remember with.
The picture is iffy, aslant, an experiment
no one can predict. Midas, the garden, a day
reaching down, shaking out the rugs,
preparing for that which cannot be prepared.
Beyond the dark window two uneven stars
wink, as if to tell their version.
Good-bye amethyst ring! Good-bye *wink wink.*
To see the underside of a moth
is to see desire's blind spot.

From its nodding, cool agenda, from its scheme
laminated under an arch, its mossy bank,
veritable and deft, comes *the song
of the already sung.* And the dream's
harsh competitor strays from its seal, as when
in the full gauzy glare of summer
we lose our way, fold our T-shirts and tents,
walk through the hinged light
until the terms
founder on familiar bedrock.
What do you know?
Even maps betray us where the fold
tears just along the tiny road we need
to get where we are going, so that in this primitive
ritual, a summer's day, the rose is a toy,
part of the general clutter in the kids' room,
part of the nameless, broken debris.

And yet, most reckless things
are beautiful in some way, you once said.
We can each think of examples.
Once you get used to the fact that
life is what you are doing moment by moment, you
just might want to try it. Cat stays out all night.
An old man who knows only his name
wanders away from his vestigial home,
sits on a bench, enters the woods.
No one he ever knew knows him now.
Gus. Nathan. Arthur. Jim.
The night's ingenuity lures him, its
nidulant cool throat
inhaling space
back to its origin, its seed
under time's rock, nest high
in the sky's bough.
Rewind. Rewind. Forget. Forget.
And the hand reaches into this story
to strangle the old man in his sleep.
Cut and print.

       But the day
returns to wean us of disparity, so we must
succumb to the sleek portion of its radius.
Why cheat ourselves, why not continue down the stairs
and Jill come tumbling after? We are turned
away from our confessions, told
to stay where we are. But I go (as I go) down,
into the spectacle, under the risen,
where the throat is stampeded with want's
insistent example: how do you like it? like this?
in the doorway, the map spreading its wings,
counting its means, denying the outcome,
famished, enflamed

                              and the mind
gathers its weather, beseeching,
undaunted, song
started and stopped:
what is the name for this condition?
What in the world have you found out?

FOR EXAMPLE (5):
SONG OF THE ALREADY SUNG

1.

The situation is not going to change.
Which situation?

Anecdote of the moon.
Held there, cast in a blitz of lopsided gas.

Or say a row of trash cans.
Something set to music, then lost.

Four wasps on a sill; some stench.
The last thing said. Say that.

Smoke inert, leaves
frozen at June.

To do with a lock
with the other side of a bridge with

another familiar strand of hair.
The body's epilogue: *not you.*

The confession stone turned
before the applause.

2.

Because it reminds me of amber.
Funny how you move them from something, the bones.

The bugs that you find in amber.
They don't look like real bones.

The something of time past—of someone working
as if they were all broken, like the mugs—

has gone awry like Icarus in his machine.
But you want to hold on, a fondness

tentative, not followed through.
Different theatrical situations

whose absurdity doesn't lead the mind
anywhere right now. More complex

replicas. Diagrams. Maybe fossils.
The amber piece, the photograph

that won't change. Speak
of another kind of time

pressing flowers in a book to
remind you of what you don't have—

controlling the bones. Each has such—
I mean an example is a sound.

The tip of it, a
very extended kite.

The challenge of the thing.
An average pen, for example.

Its relationship to these
pieces of light: the smallest piece.

Is it a model?
It doesn't touch bottom.

A distinct velocity, a
quivering line when

absence of color becomes color's
harmonic particularity in air.

A lot about America:
real people, real objects

fashions in color, partial statements;
a meandering, vagrant line.

3.

In the midst of a phantom inch
wild and beautiful simultaneous competing tunes
an immense scattering
to picture dissonance
among the rushes
this excerpt
the horror of our kind
say an image, facedown,
never to be lifted
touched for the sake of it
the shine

and those who are not clumsy
the advantage of that
yes scooping water from a pond
child with broken net
standing at the threshold maybe

As someone's father
elicits recurrent gaps
net of the fallen through
of the unrecovered
attached to that
singing that tune
between desire and the actual
a theory of response
the spectator's knowledge
now's edge
inscribed, instructed to sing
that lullaby again
tell a story
put the sock on the doll
pull the dress up over her head
immersed in yellow
iconicity of a scream.

4.

The situation
is not going to change. Refrain
etched above the song.
Erudition of a rat.
Mind of a turbine engine.
Luck of the draw.
Examples of what?

To watch as the reference

floats away. Away
as nightmare or game.
Glancing across the table at another's—
the confusion distance is.
A beseeching gap as in a harbor
or panels left uncertain, occupied by
weather. What cannot be
transformed into something else.

Another in another room.
It's a bright day in a small Egyptian town
but the birds here are nervous.
I can hear her voice
but I don't know what she is saying.
A time and place for circular action: this
ends in some kind of secret
some kind of occasion
an abandoned pier
the far end of a pier
alone at the far end of a pier
some kind of bargain is drawn up
an occasion for meeting
face to face.

Downstairs, downstairs

a person decides.
Talking to myself (himself) this
basement in retrospect is mine.
I am always installed on a still point
a potentially dangerous spot
a seed bed

I can build sexual fantasies.
                    Maybe
I can say good-bye.

A clean white space but no space is neutral.
Thumbprints. Something to
acknowledge, bring back, shadow
thrown out, cast, dragged across the gravel
repeatedly. Wanting all said all done
to save one or two—
an urge to get up, go.
No particular creed, the girl now walking
across the grass, some pages in her left hand,
I can't say what in her right.
No space is neutral. There's a man
a kind of cult figure, a kind of hero.
Sound is a replacement for him (me).
A house is what everyone knows by heart.

Then the real is a convincing show? Of course
the beam looks real, but is more melancholy
an inhalation of breath moving across
to a charged little image.
It's like looking at a forest
through the eye of a needle.
In a shop I found a dirty white vase. I washed it;
now it is clean.
There's a form of dreaming in another form
and there's the sacredness of common objects.

FOR EXAMPLE (6):
OF THE FIRE

to Michael Palmer

These many mouths leave us vagrant, unsuited.
Bring in some jazz, or a sleuth
amiably fixated
on postage. There's a welter here
and accidents have happened
among revisionist families not yet indicted
by the variegated stalks of what will be known as
this year. Sooner or later all affinities
will be yielded to the public sphere, our
search ended. The light revoked,
jumping from the dish—newt, preacher, trip—
none of us can measure in the trick webbing
called talk. Not enough spit
to ease the muttering ensemble or train
back on track as the mouth is carved
into its rind.
    But then the reprehensible world
begins its testimony, verifying the impersonal
like a slate on which nothing has been written.
Glue untested in the sieve, and here
the tick of a stranger's bookcase
after the fire (referring back to it)
           its field's
chamber of elisions/sky
wearing a tarp or dark lens
aimed at noon over noon waters, ephemeral purpose
unchained from the harbor's expectations

as the Architect of Destruction builds a cavern
hectic with tarnish. That night you could see
geometries of skeletal reason—doorways, plinths—
left in the set of the empty set
(soldiers excused now from representation
because we had not seen that war) idle furnace
over there away from us
in the exclusionary rights of what we wage
in the gravity of what we know
or do not, duration mothering her child who sleeps
in bed under the sovereign roof in the moon's lamé light.
Fire, feeding on night, moving through

        and swans!

        the ardor of it, a design
        ignited well past the sun

        now cosseted in passing
        particular bit
        of something else

        in front of the pattern
        being quick on the stair, many sing

        impeccable Florence desired as a
        woodshop and the small

        weeps back, we its matrix
        in eight sections, like journalism

there was
a blue hospital, red sweater, steel towers, malice.

To ask

> *by my/until her/in a dream/to the hold*
> *of consciousness/at a sunlit/in the unsaid*
> *in a flicker/for/by her*
> *of a deaf/of snow.*
> *To the pink/in reverence*
> *in her bed/before Easter/with Moses/on the edge*
> *until we/of his wood box/at winter's/to her*
> *on the noon/from the sky.*

                              Together we have come
to this side of the bridge
and stared past it, the boys
walking on ahead their long shadows mingled
thruway to thruway and past all the glass
ejected into the glimpse: call it that, that or them.
Animation trapped on the surface, like print.
But then the Gentleman with Country Hair
appears in Miami, obscurely thematic.
He admonishes us for staring at our service
and picks up his shoes invisibly pitched—
black, black on black—all this in the river below.
Objects come round to their slogans
too arbitrary or too ornate and he calls the cat
Salem after a cigarette. (Everything not seen is
parenthetical. Night is always parenthetical, for example.)
Whatever became of the ashes? Down on the rug
the origin is in small print
and the first sound in the garden is there also
humming and rhythmical, its transparent plume
rising.

        To gain a mercantile blue in a catalogue of blues, its
habitual, standard, issue

already squandered on expedience: nothing to be
launched. But what do I know?
I am merely a tourist here
in the Year of the Broken Hat, have not learned
how to bow like wheat in wind, do not know
which lucidity keeps the key
while inviting another in, making a sequence.
The thing—call it *horse* or *gorse* or *force*—
appears as nomenclature only, and there's a fine
upstanding pier lengthening our stay
sorting the mathematics out to keep it afloat
under plastic hail on plastic slats.
I cannot look at myself through the eyes of others
so cannot speak for them. If someone were to ask, I'd say

                                        blue-gray November light
                lapping at sand, pale
                pinkish rocks, grass
                molting to rust, leaves
                paper weight, stillness
                facing advent
                small boat eroding a path, swans—

                A train
                parts one space from another, and a figure, a man
                or woman, there's an embrace, awkward, arms
                in too many places, encumbered, helping with stuff
                saying *how was your trip you look great glad you came.*
                The world still more beautiful than thought, heron
                low over water to show us what silence really is.

Ear to ground tells of the future, leaf on roof
reflects an opposing window's glare
as the immoderate convert comes to rest in sloth shade.
But are these surfaces to be trusted

in the hooligan now—cull, impede, dissolve—
when so many strange darlings
are ready to subvert all margins of error?
Is this a body speaking, or just
an oceanic drone come to be tamed?
To inhale such episodic smoke you must
transgress its maker, filtered up into clustered heaven
where gold trim circles the amorous
unimpeded there. Until

> *of radiant competition/on the lower/for my peaceable*
> *on my shirt/on the grove*
> *in nature's wood/in stately despair/by white of ark*
> *in today's/for consumption/on the dark night*
> *in the dark*
>   *for being themselves/in despondency*
> *on my space/out of my mouth/in the thing*
> *in the salt/to wisdom/of the dragonflies*
> *off instantly/of the surroundings/of the bearded tongue/in us*
> *of paradise/in profusion/about Heraclitus/in the crowd*
> *on nutshells/of mud/on the edge/before any excess/without limit*

Humming a tune, the heiress flees
in a flare of publicity, her amulet
or headdress tilted awkwardly,
straps twisted, green shoe torn at the heel.
Free at last, she arrives breathless
to see what the artist has done to the pool.
Many sons earlier, she had let herself
down into one of her own devising, putting
wonder to the test. Trial unto me these
watery chains, bleach my hair, condone
this lattice-work of twigs. I shall stay
in the gesture for as long as it takes
even as the fire encroaches on the very blue

we decided not to buy. The umbrella
cannot shield us from the flames.
Do not give away what you intended to keep;
do not keep what you intended to give freely
or you might find yourself impaled on the wind
footloose as a saint, your address-book
scattered into the soot-filled air.
Lake project, pool improvement, water system
all are things of the past
                              through which the Greek sailor
traversed to become a coin.
Above, on that other cloud,
children run through their amazed magics
inventing as they go, their skills unforeseen.
Even the wisest of us cannot read
but for next year's introduction
in the ballet chamber's endowment: chicken
encrusted with nuts, ballerinas wire-thin.
O but the minister hath committed adultery!
O but the senator is twitching on the dais!
Luckily, we have the means
to recover from this surge of unnatural weather:
fire, flood, fire, wind
pitching houses to abstraction, hell
on the screen. A pantomime of ribbons
unfurls from a nonexistent spool. The fire spread.
When the clouds broke, you could see
the litigating flames had sentenced the hills
to anonymity. Gather your deeds
and your next of kin, they had advised, even
as a cold child came into the world with a purpose.

FOR EXAMPLE (7):
AND THE FIRE SPREAD

In case the world
changes, in
case things stampede im-
patiently into view/all
arms expectant and the arcade
slings through plasticity an awed spell/in
case this is legible and we are lucky and present not
nearly asleep/not still in the
after you've gone/in case
lesions open and the manifest swells to be copied—

"everything that comes

my way becomes a picture for me
of what I am thinking about at the time"—

bride

wrapped in rags doused with kerosene
goes enflamed into dusk
drawing the long fog
after her into waters where

of hope/of rapture
against a distinction/in traveling/with nothing
for eternity/in ambush/for one/in the hope
of an endless/of capture/of song/for a stranger
in the midst/to a certain/on it/to whom/to whom
to a doubt/of being/of guilt/in the tree
in the valley/of triumph

for two sticks/of how/fallen into/of kisses
on her lap/to the future/in my shoes/out of spinning
for the same/with my stuff/of a morning/to this

                                                            what is
keeps custody of what we will never be
clustered radically in knots
withheld as lateness or shine, its
webbed course stayed. Nothing speaks so there is no
poetry there, just
riot and tidal wisps
blown into shade
and other sham effusions
                                    (except when otherwise
alone, although we are now
rhetorically cold, flimsy
as gloves left on a doorstep)—do not, even then,
agree.

            "For the clarity that we are aiming at
is indeed complete clarity, which means that the
problems should disappear completely.
The real discovery is one that gives peace, that
no longer brings itself into question. We
demonstrate a method by examples
and the series of examples can be broken off."

All is contained in the bubble's floating code,
not this sheltering skin
with its abrasions.
The lovely conduct of things—architectural, denuded—
seen from above, is elsewhere conditioned
but open to surmise. Here,
in the throat's watery plume, a voice

is besieged by the moon's portrait, mistress
of the huge marquee where the dots are not connected
and of the curve's tree, the river's city, its theme
drawn into a bowl as color's allegiance.

Three doves perch against a plaster sky.
Lichen steal from tapestries and maps.
A pewter flood.

                    What is the world
if not brilliance tarnished to memorable debris?
Toothless, repugnant, Our Lady of Hags
drags from coast to coast her burlap bag
leaking. *O moon!* we call, *O bright thing!*
Who are we to arrest serendipity
when your radiance
dribbles into the sea? The captain's skill
did not save the crew, flaws
foiled passage so what was expected
did not arrive on the stainless steel tray.
Something axiomatic or idiomatic
flew out of the cuckoo's beak and away
into the century we can almost see.
Huge calipers moved against wind,
doses of prior delight, suds 'n tubs,
gleeful memoirs of an awful age.
Stoic vouchers, burdens of proof—

                         Meanwhile,
a vanguard carried
estrangement into the path of our alliance, and
pandemonium's tryst skyrocketed into the voyeur's polished lens.
Tools of trade. A fashion for linen
sheathed our hands, legs, heads
into fake burdens; bleach

made our eyes smart with revision.
Confidence thus augmented, even the wind
seemed irresponsible—no vacancy at the empty inn
and the fire spread. Dissertations multiplied
into the quixotic chat of the living dead,
figurines conversed on rooftop gardens
like balconies of gods. *Tear here; cut along
this edge.* Above a broken cauldron
something wept
staining the windows with filigrees of ash.

Caprice in the name of following when nothing, as nothing,
beckons, although our service is still best,
sending the mediated village gruel.
If you, in tawdry remembrance, lamp-lit, were
to come in at last
would you still carry a tune? How long
before the mood comes to rest as in an earlier now
preserved as curious mirth? *What is it?*
Paper umbrellas collect distant rain.
This close to failure
a runt god might flip out of the drain
to rescue us. Tiny gold hip flask; atomic
cuff links. And that president's grin
never to be endured again
in any language. What's in store for us today,
what catalogue, what bequest? Curtains
spill out onto the sky to hide
a cast of strangers: no machine, no team, no
fat white shoes with good arch support,
just the cold noise of the eternally unhomed.

She gazes from every glossy page,
a slender emptiness. How many stairs
has she climbed to nowhere?

Morning, then, is a mask? And these songs, they?
Toys to prevent vertigo.
Tell me a really scary story, catch this
wild mimosa ball plucked from Blake's reel
(Have you practiced your absence today?)
or some twist of fate the scavengers provide
to tool the future as patterns of wind
braid *the last person to be executed in Florida*
was a black slave with the news.
Take heed. Safety in numbers is a hoax.
One man's guide is another's
mistranslation, stumbling
barefoot down the cliff
into the cartoon's inky crawl.

                              Of its own success
upon the asylum/of course/into something/for
repressively/of patients/to five or six hundred
of that sort/on the edge/on all sides
from the semantic/against moral treatment/with it
by a growing population/of an organic
of the twentieth century/in understanding/by contrast
of decay/on their part/in institutional
of an infectious illness/of sanity/into some fun.

Devotional excess laminates the seal.
Facsimile's burlesque obscures the song.

How unseemly our ambassadors.
Could not relax. Could not pull loose.

I carry my skyline with a harsh tip,
an old-fashioned fountain
held by spirits even
after the funeral, so the monastery's sink
is in the center with a logic

behind birds. The birds are necessary
if the dawn is to be useful.
And the enemy suddenly from city to city
comes forward toward the lover
with a frame, an animal, and finds a way
by touch through the drawingroom into the field
pressing down the fire escape by flashlight—

Traipse from island to island with nothing to sell.
Head back to the cabin's shade.

Do it. Leave here. Take your
empirical tirade with you, its grandeur as winter
and zigzag prow, missing person's voice.
Even in gossip's vacant lot
there's a trace of each of us in every buyout.
Of a person/in profile
of space/toward you
of floors/to live/between/from a box
with gold/of a bird/of a man/of its oracle
into different/of a content/between objects
of an ideal.
My hands
in the shape of a house.
Where's the kitchen, where forbearance?
Lost antecedents, faces in another century
when photography is not allowed.
Sell the groom his trousers.
Then I recalled that his buttons
were but partial moons,
and the waterwheels in the cellar
became extinct, or so we were told.

Not in the room with the fake hair's
baleful expertise, not

where the sister is
in the parapet's transition
that others cannot hear, not
the imperious yank
into hoodlum's fame where delusion accrues,
not the hum's drag across limelight
where company is sometimes kept
as tidal mirrors break light.
Could we say this green is humorless
and shines only to please,
an acrobat's poised flip?
Is the postcard delirious
with its orphaned stamp—you go
your way, I'll go mine—the evening
uncollected, a penny on the street?
What is unfinished is not by choice,
gathering inconvenient slang
to ride the large dark over the dark city.
I can see this thing opening onto another thing
but I cannot pronounce it,
neither the one with the frieze of antlers
nor the one with the clocks. Taking off gloves
is a theatrical event, like tossing a pail of water
at an immense flame
or following a script in which a boy
impales himself on a mast as the crowd watches.
The crowd always watches.

> *On the walls/in the starkest/in the wrong*
with our physical/of fire/on fire
to the Hebrews/of plans/of sins
without the/in this century
in a revelation/on the other hand/in this century/to a
perception/at least/for a moment/for us
in which/of the relation/from the great/between

surfaces/of experience/in every/of their
to their diction/to each/between surfaces
in a forward/from which/by myself/into my innermost
by my soul's/with love/in a region
with my eye/above my mind/before the light
with love/into an awareness/with love
from you/in time/out of which features
for forces/of something/by mismanagement/from his face
of information/on the soundtrack.

ASHES, ASHES

MISSING AGES

to Kenward Elmslie

1.

At times dry weight shifts vicariously on mental limbs like music
hurting remotely.

At times, fathers die and die, but
biography is a false persuasion.

Inhaling the night I am stitched to you
with incendiary sorrow.

A party? In costume, you say, and
invited to dwell in a sea of lords and ladies?
Quit smoking? Weep?
And those magnolias, are they
part of the wall, or of the rushing river
with its vestal gashes arriving on a whim of connective tissue, on air?

In a foreign land we will learn some songs.
They will last as long as the next gold rush.

2.

                    This is my résumé. Hire me.
I am from January, where the winds are severe.
I am an immigrant from evening, hire me.

My father was a sweeper of secrets, a silk merchant
in Vienna, he had no boots, he had no lotion for his skin.
Hire me. This handkerchief is woven from ninety percent.
My daughters are in Mexico on a jaunt. They have not
read of the insurrection, they
do not get CNN. This is my black scarf. This is my painting of a jar.
Hire me. This is a photo of my husband
taken when he was a young man in jail.
I still remember sex, I can tell you stories
of such women you will invite me to your trial. The snow
stinks of yellow. Someone in a corner says thank you repeatedly.
Hire me. I am what you do not know and will not miss.

3.

The rapacious sky is as a winged figure
flaunting its rapture, a film
of film whose beginning middle and end
we will never see. Knowledge is form.
Wait for me under the apple tree on the blue sand.
A discordant glue travels into courage, and the cut
speeds along the finger's edge. Weather
confounds our dreams, we wake humid
with what we forgot while those who stay late
sleep in the margins, fools
for fools' gossip. Millions are spent
on regular episodes from that life.
Starved monks subsume an awful
delay, snowbound, iconoclastic, their
amnesia intact. I was a gallant trooper
through the history of Nordic exploration,
I sank heavy water.
I wear the soiled increment
as a shield; my eyes break day by day

in sublime iteration: unbearable choice among peers.
We speak in tongues, yes?
All instances fill and empty as
the suction of love plays that rule, coming to stay
in the habits of an angel skinned by disbelief.
He raises the issue to emblematic stature:
nature loves a plague as much as a rose.

4.

The mutant veracity of almost.
The steep incline of a heart.
The doted line of convention.
The little afterlife of hazard.
What spills from the mouth of a passionate dog.
The voice of reason, its ineptitude with layers.
The amulets of thieves; grief as such.
The occasion purloined.
A brother's best scarf.
A brother's gray scarf.
Between best and gray, an analogy.
Icon of an ordinary okay.
Between nine and fine.
The makeshift bed.
The national interest.

5.

Which from among these absences will you choose?
When the French girl arrives, no one
will answer the phone for a week.
If I were invited to sleep over, I would bring

my dowsing rod, over which
you could say your prayers, but if we
touch the beautiful soul it will
never stop raining.
One by one, we are announced, and our
names are a weightless carriage.
Hire me. I live on the stairs. I go up and down.

HARM'S WAY, ARM'S REACH

1.

Things are not cured by resilience.
Thrash thrash wept the amputated limb
unable to lean, starved of its hair.

A group of men
wanted to avenge
to trunacte the city/to make everyone
scream.
        On the bateau, in wild heat
children laughed through the history lesson
through the great facades in the Year of Friendly Fire.

The friend looked away
subverting fate
             (because of the wound)
saying *I disapprove of*
the personality of the street
which cannot be arranged. Henceforth,
two out of three curtains must be closed.

In fiction's unhinged seat
in the hesitant new

resting under a shadow
unbodied in febrile need

and from afar, far in that land
song of the first bird

pressure in the throat
gospel devoted to mercy

a zone or hinge
out of the discursive enclosure

long frieze of furious goddesses
wrath of the drunken boy

in the Home for Depraved Girls
in the Department of Recent Arrivals.

2.

                              My name is an unsolved
equation I come toward you
                              I ask you to meet me
at twilight in the unfinished part of the story
in the small grotto in the room with giraffes
and a man with a string
                              when it is raining
when all the maps are spread on the desk
where the towels/where the nest fell
                              I write to you
from the place of habit but today I am young
I am merely a slant perpetually drawn
into spelling
              My name is a tall man
who walks along the Street of Books
in the Year of the Mouth who has not forgotten
how to kiss

The friend says
but in order to fix it

you must have a sense of
prior perfection she says *light beauty fire* I say
toward and *rage of the weed* and *etymology* and *starvation.*
I say the change or revolution which does not produce
the conclusion or final event

                          catastrophe as definition
                          the wall that was.

3.

Where we come from
abides as choice

it is the way of avowal.

Have you remembered to take all your belongings with you?
Today all distance is summer.

If you open the curtains you will see
the evil wires the broken lock the rifles
the plot
          dark crevices of diminished weight
the lesson of the open hand your mother's maiden name.
You will hear
                a cluster of pilgrims undaunted by speed
flagrant as any transparency
the indelible scheme of the wish
a parade for no reason
                          an apricot thud where the limb was.

ASHES, ASHES
(ROBERT RYMAN, SUSAN CRILE)

1.

Humped gravity/tree-backed vatic shard/white
disarray/arc
        secretly allied to the dark clear dark/herald
sick of his forms, dry
with remorse.

There is a cup in the landscape buried under the indefinite
as if it would last: salt, sugar, salt.
Sooner or later he'll want a child
hushed up against him
spawned in egregious thirst. Pale
inventory of a lunar smile/applause track
slips off the rails, flute twisted, strings
knotted and loose. Must be numbers, letters,
afloat on the surface: augur, thread, mast,
honeycomb, terrace.

I am jealous of his garment, his shirt's wide cut
the gaudy transience crouched in his throat,
great thimble of heat poured out—

a thing in the landsacpe:
salt, sugar, salt.

2.

Now this news.
If you do not mention it she will not cry.
I laughed as well at the child's invention.
Yesterday I saw a painting
of a young woman in a red dress. Yesterday

yesterday I saw
paintings of fire. I met a woman she said
my father my father my father
and as she spoke he became her portrait.

If a room is artificially white
all whisper in the affirmed
physical space: scraps of
touch touching touch.

The violinist moves
like a marionette/his
legs buckle/hair
jumps with light/torso

breaks forward.
Music adheres
enclosing the figured silence
as if setting were bondage.

As if setting were bondage
and we on the brink had walked up to it/raw thread
chafing the waters of the percolating wave.
As if we could say to the fire,

Stop! I command you, stop!

3.

That night the moon was the Evil Banana King
crouched in a bowl.

See, said the child, drawing the light,
this is The Princess I asleep on her bed

this her pet snake/this
is the mother in her slip
she is wearing a nest on her head
she is a long lady standing in front of a leaky mirror
she says I would rather be in jail than
hidden in these devotions

I am making red and yellow stitches
although my crayons are stale.

Now she is walking toward a cave
where the tools are hidden and the Book of Instruction,
peeled into slight wings, batters the foam.

This is a circle.
The name of the circle is Gray Pond.
There are lilies on the pond/you cannot see them
as if the memorial had rubbed away.

This is the ghost.

4.

This black thing is a mistake.
It could be a cat or a cart.

It is lonely like a mouth in a desert
under sand. I

do not know who hears it.
I do not know who calls.

It is a long way since
with no way out into a song.

There is an ecstasy in battle,
on the somber chasm's edge.

That thou woudst narrate me
thru these worlds.

I am in derelict garb
my category is broken

I am covetous of the extreme.

5.

Then the periphery dawned as later, as ebb tide
on a channel, as the gray pond of recognition,
the memorial rubbed into a wall.
How soon? you ask, and again, How soon?
You may as well ask is the water bloody
is the chair frail.
                    And, at the horizon, a ribbon of fire
finds its way to the woman's dress to ravish it so in the box
wild ashes fly about in a litter of silence.
The father-woman and the child do not meet, the
violinist never smiles. Is it merely a sunset, this fire,

seen from the dusty window of a passing train, or is it
the oiled conflagration of an event brought home to us as a trophy:
which comes first, artifact or source,
and what stroke stokes the flame?

WHEN COLOR DISAPPOINTS (JOSEPH BEUYS)

to Paul Shullenberger

1.

Something must have lifted our spirits
caused our tongues to be untied
dreamed us from ruin
where the ur-bells begin

                              sun

roiled under an elk's body
penciled toward or into its subject
willing to aspire

as the turbulent same
doubles its augur   "body color"   "blood"

These (unnamed, above)
have a gash or surprise, a smile
missing the dangling thing as the tacit
crosses over to where meanings are
                                   mind

changing again into its mystery
flume of song and cedars made to weep
across from the flags in the signature gardens
trajectory of a fragment at all times in view

—meet me in the designer collection
—there's a limit here how white is your hair?
—are you, were you ever, afraid?

Tulipe noire and fat stain
below street level in the currency of paper

wrinkled ribs of light
bicoastal war
cross retrieved from snow
boy listening for red, hearing its cure

Partita of leaves
as a desire for evidence, heroic esplanade
of the remnant museum, so the morbid thing
anchors a panoply of *yes*, including
a swan

Something must have diverted our pain

This painting has been re-
moved during the re-
hanging of the Second Floor Lounge Please
excuse the vacant space it will re-
placed as soon as possible

Grammar of Lincoln's eyes
biweekly take-home essays

Speaking from within a secret
filament dissembling, the tongue's
ardent, literal wish

calendar awkwardly re-
newed: old field, old damage

said to come true as any interlude must.

2.

In a further stripe iconoclast mode which
jiffy to   roiling haphazard
from   All these beginnings
printed askew, a pattern
quietly revealed over insurmountable   Sense
closes over what   to be
                    heavy   on film.
The motel's windows open onto a hall of
onto an American   all predecessors
            native tile. I have come
      these names, as to say, these
preferences, one shore over   one
skeletal phrase   emulating
its hearer.

Something withstood?
Something shattered?

How crowd
            into   lent forsythia
raging   the fill anonymous
                  the blinking obscene
as
    the committee in absentia.
                              Now
mirrored
bricks do travel   schemes

rest in the archive,
stamp on the screen. It matters
less in another language

captured, reproduced as
in space.

The classic range incalculably slit.

Old zero range to which nothing comes back.
Later, when doubling ceases, lines,
spells, whatever. So the earth has its day,
phantom chant, surf. Such
listening requires ammunition: a brag, an
apology, syntactical praise. Something roots
the sound's principle, rinsing lesions
recorded by evening   insects,
other dry apparitions unthwarted by grass.

3.

An avenue of wool, karate, gap
hectic magics swell into magnolias
gracefully aloft
                head of a woman
posing for it, vehemently caught
the incursion stilled thus—
autonomous migrant persons
retained as sight

                And the arriving spectacle
reflected as half of any width
mountains of calls whose voices are not

not rain, not music, not the deed recalled
not any *is* filtered through time.

Completing the fragment, lasting that long.

                    So assume the perdition of
answers, asking the clock
now trailing after his vestments
responsibly repressesd, dare to conceal
the way girls are said to, weaving shadows
into flesh, refuting his stare

so the motif is instructive
borrowed from
the universal real

gesture true to itself
leaf or stroke

                    ugly gold–like thing
                    shuttering bough.

4.

I have imagined something urgent is happening
imagined I am awake

I recall the bitter neon kingdom
patina of sentient beings, reversal of gloss

I think his fingers touched this fat book
where all secrets are told

man off to an assignation
woman in wait

I think his ears hear
blame on the radio

                          a bit of thunder recorded in another country
news of a solo   The instruments she makes have
extremely long   thirty or
                      played by rubbing the hand along extremely long
resonances   I   it is a pleasurable excursion

I have come to see
your ladder, cane, hat
the tear at the back of your knees
your name that belongs to others
so I say it not to you

the falling motif of the twilight
bells, many bells
some were bells
they may have been bells.

IN THE MUSEUM OF THE WORD
(HENRI MATISSE)

to Thomas Neurath

1.

There was the shield of another language
transient enclosure/gate
                swings open
shut shut
       walking unnoticed into it
                   as with *avec*
down stone steps into the vineyard
         rose as decoy/beauty as use
      riding up onto the the surface
               glance, sway/hawk
comes down dragging silence with it
no light, no applied Sun King

               opposing shine, commonly
               bereft
                   creature of habit lost in a wood.

Here I said take these thimbles these hooks
you can count them and toss them away
one six nine/they
will fit under any stream, fill any slot
will color the waters
of the restless exhibit
             lizard's billowing throat
        hiccups on a wall/its tongue

flicks air

                              bird-strewn wind.

And the milkman's doubling dream, his
dilemma, the composition of his
intolerance for dawn/great
Aubergine Interior too frail to move: link
between Conversation and event. There was

there had been an awkward tour.

I was shown two rivers, their vistas

                              snailfooted/waterskinned abyss
                              wheelwinged staring at muck
                              weedy, indifferent, purplepronged up
                              in avid rays/their comprehensive is
                              bearing emblems smaller than time

under the decor
coiled among rocks

I met a woman with odd eyes
she said this is the figure of guilt
hurling a snake boulder

                    wall

ripped from a wall

                              fragment installed.

This country is a
cavern of drunk light/shade rubbed onto day
the corpse is not luminous/vines dangerous/flowers profuse

as in an arbitrary Eden. These
consolations also are damaged/seepage under roofs
thru which the musics
might come.

2.

She traveled.

Sun lay against her knees printed on purple
boughs fell with a thrash
color collected on the dusty sea floor
                              fronds meticulously scissored/commerce
                raged thru the sky binding its harmonies
regardless of space.

Although something insisted, pointing.
Although similar doors did not open similarly.
Blackbirds reminded her of written blackbirds/it was
humid with blackbirds/her mind an inscription/a proverb
or heap so she could almost see its faithful
retrieval/monkey hanging with long limbs/bird
on her shoulder/rigid man/moon
doubled in glass.

Nothing timid is allowed while we believe in it.
Doubtless it should be told.
Doubtless tools will be needed.
Desire in an etched wineglass like an old bloody dime.

3.

A fable of prescience/looking up into the sky's garden
and the statues on the roof
withstanding bombardment

        seven paces to Paradise
            halted startled voyagers
                the possible direction collides with the way
                    each morning's tray a rudimentary splendor.

I said here are some useful numbers
some untranslatable rain

        facades pockmarked in the new contingent state
          now untethered on the Street of the Harp
            the blind man cannot/soft sloped palm
              dog leading him on into the unscented garden

They are scooping out the bloods in jars
the real has a stench/ it is not
the tableaux we elicit.

I went up a steep hill in a foreign country
in unknown grass/there was an aperture

        boats, birds
              many unknown letters
          snake-wrapped urn
                  Persephone
                    stolen, raped
Hotel where Mozart stayed/street where Brecht
Beckett's daily walks

        impermanent oracular trace so that
not any fragment will do counting my steps

from margin to margin/scenic on foot
turning a page.

4.

In Museum Street, Liu Hai is
standing on a three-legged toad

the toad
was thought to inhabit the moon

it lost its leg
in order to correspond

with the three-legged bird
that inhabits the sun.

And the Apostles were fishermen and thieves
base fellows neyther of wit nor worth

                seal
         reduced to a wax turd
            flaunting a tail
                      charred Charter's remains

                            displayed under glass.

Merlin
helps a young man
to paint his
shield/an illustration

Attendants in a garden mounted on a crane

Under green and ochre glazes
under turquoise purple and ochre glaze
with aubergine, green and straw glazes

In a woods a black scroll
let us caption the first scene

on oak
on poplar on lime

green earth has been used under gold leaf
instead of the usual orange bole

as well as I can

      As if conducted to the eulogy fields to lie down with a shade
      under turbulent vines
      walls studded
      Peiro's meticulous plumage

Come this way said the guard this is where
your opponent lies grieving

here are the spoils set in violent maps, re-
named, disinhabited, inherited, made
bloodless with shine.

Read this example
it praises the country of origin

teaches you facts
in the new gray wing

                        lion, corpulent monk

Here are some postcards to send home/the one
you want is sold out/the thing you came to see
is temporarily gone

           that she is seated/that the door
           that the window
           that she wears part of a tree
           that the color of the conversation
           moves as if it were sky/that the frame
           continues to dissolve
           (sadness of the Rose Marble Table)
           man wearing a pajama column
           rigidly pronounced/woman
           redrawn in response—

           Is it possible to memorize this blue?

Diana Michener

ABOUT THE AUTHOR

Ann Lauterbach lives in New York, where she is a professor at the City College and the Graduate Center. She is also head of the writing faculty in the M.F.A. program at Bard College. The author of *Many Times, But Then; Before Recollection; Greeks;* and *Clamor,* she has received grants from the New York State Council for the Arts, the Guggenheim Foundation, and Ingram Merrill. In 1993, she was a recipient of the prestigious John D. and Catherine T. MacArthur fellowship.

PENGUIN POETS